Contents

Hurricane

Selina was looking out of the school window.

"Look at those trees," she thought. The wind was so strong that the trees bent right over. She looked up. Big grey clouds were running across the sky.

"Stop work and listen, children," said the teacher. Suddenly Selina knew what she was going to say.

"A hurricane is coming," said the teacher. "There's been a telephone message. No more school today."

Everyone in the Caribbean knew what to do when a hurricane came. It was a good idea to be at home out of danger then.

Selina and her little brother Bobby lived near to the school.

"Will we be all right, Selina?" asked Bobby, as they ran along the road. This was the first hurricane to hit their island for a long time.

"Yes," said Selina. "Hurry, Bobby. Let's get inside. Here comes the rain."

At home, Mum had just come back from work.

"Come and help me, Selina," she called. Selina could only just hear her voice over the wind. "Help me to board up this window." A hurricane can blow all the windows out if you don't board them up.

"Is Dad here?" asked Bobby.

"He's gone off in the truck to fetch Grandma," said Mum.

They helped Mum to take food down into the cellar under the house. Dad had made their cellar and it was very strong. They would be out of danger there.

"Switch on the radio, Bobby," said Mum. A voice on the radio said,

"The hurricane is coming, but keep calm. Keep calm and don't go out."

"But Dad and Grandma are out –" Selina began to say, but just then, the door opened and they came in.

Now that everyone was together, Selina did feel calm.
They all sat in the cellar, playing games with Bobby and
trying to listen to the radio through the noise of the
wind. It was blowing and screaming round their house
like an animal, Selina thought. Like an animal screaming
in pain.

"Will it blow our roof away?" Bobby asked.

"No," said Grandma. "But even if it did, we would still
be all right, Bobby."

It went on for a long, long time, the wind screaming and the rain roaring and roaring on the roof. Suddenly the light went out.

"Oh no," said Selina. She was frightened.

"Never mind," said Grandma. "It'll be all right in the morning. You'll see. It's time to sleep now."

"Sleep? In this noise?" asked Selina.

The next thing Selina knew, it was morning.

She turned over. Everything was full of light.

"Mum?" she said.

"Up here, Selina," Mum called. "Come and look.
The hurricane has gone. The sun is shining again."
Selina got up and went to look.

"Oh, Mum!" she said.

Trees had crashed down everywhere. One had only
just missed their truck. Across the road, every house had
lost its roof.

"We have been lucky," said Mum. "So lucky. Our
house is all right this time."

"Let's try to drive Grandma home," said Dad. "We'll see how her house got on."

He had to drive very slowly. In some places the rain had washed the road away. The river had come right up and the bridge had gone. Up on the mountains, most of the trees had been knocked down by the wind. And then Grandma said,

"Oh no! It's gone! My house has gone! And all my banana trees as well!"

The hurricane had knocked down everything. Her little house had been turned right over. The hurricane had gone off across the Caribbean, still blowing.

They got out of the truck.

"What can I do?" asked Grandma. She looked very sad.

"Look," said Selina. Some people were coming.

"Need any help?" asked a woman.

"We'll soon put some new banana trees in," said a man.

"And we'll get your house right," said another. "It'll soon be as good as new."

Grandma looked at everyone. "Will it?" she asked.

"Of course it will, Grandma," said Selina. She looked up at the clear sky. "Let's start now," she said.

Welcome to India

It was Ajay and Kamla's first day in India. They and their mother had flown in that morning from London. Now they were on their way to the village where Mum's uncle and auntie lived.

"Look!" said Ajay, as the bus went along by a river. "That looks fun." Some children were playing in a tree, laughing and jumping into the water.

"Oh yes," said Kamla. "It's so hot."

"We'll soon be there," Mum said.

At the village, everyone came running to meet them.

"Welcome, welcome," said Uncle.

"I'll take you round the village," said their cousin Satish. "Come on."

"Wait, Satish," said Auntie. "Your cousins need a rest first."

They sat in the garden and Auntie made them a lovely cold drink. Then Satish took them round to meet all his friends.

"I think I'm going to like India," said Kamla.

Soon, Satish, Ajay and Kamla were going everywhere together.

"Let's go to the market," Satish said one morning. Satish let them take turns to ride his bike, and they were at the market in no time.

"Oh, we must buy one of those whistles," said Kamla.

"Or a little red elephant," said Satish. "Or some of these cakes."

"Or a snake," said Ajay. "A snake in a basket."

Another day, Ajay and Kamla went to school with Satish. The teacher wrote in Hindi on the board, and the children copied it down. Ajay and Kamla tried to copy it too, but Hindi was hard for them to write.

"Keep trying," said the teacher, but they couldn't write beautiful Hindi like she could. Kamla's Hindi went right off the paper.

"Never mind," said Satish. "I'll do it for you."

One day, Auntie said, "A special time is coming. It's spring. That means it's time for Holi. At Holi, everyone says welcome to the spring."

Auntie and Mum began to work very hard, making special food and drink for Holi.

"That looks good," said Ajay. "I'm hungry."

"Just wait," said Auntie.

It was a long time for the children to wait, but at last everyone sat down together. How good the food was!

The next day, the children had some fun.

"Old clothes, please, Ajay and Kamla," said Mum.
At Holi you can throw powder and water at each other.
The children ran round the village, laughing and
shouting. Satish had yellow powder. Ajay had blue
powder. Kamla's powder was red. Soon, all their clothes
were yellow, blue and red.

"Oh well," said Mum. "It's not Holi every day, is it?"

At last it was time to go home. They just had one more day in India. Auntie and Uncle said they would go with them to the city to see them off. Auntie put on her best clothes and jewels for the trip. She took out her most beautiful sari.

"Look how long it is, Kamla," she said. "Now, this is how to put on a sari. We do it this way."

The city was very big and full of cars and lorries.

"Hold on to me," shouted Uncle over the noise. "Hold on to me when you cross the street."

It was exciting to be in a city again after the village. They all went on a long bus ride to see the sights, and then they went shopping.

"I'm going to buy a new sari for myself," said Mum. "Just one. Then I must look for things to give to people at home."

Soon it was time to go.

"It's sad to say goodbye," said Mum.

"You'll come back one day," said Uncle.

They went to have their picture taken together.

"Now when you look at that picture, you'll think of us here in India," said Satish. "And you won't forget us."

"We'll never forget," said Ajay.

"No, never," said Kamla. "Never, never, never!"

Christmas

Great Britain – Christmas Eve

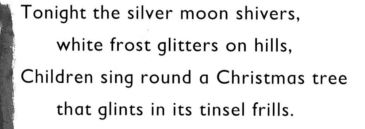

Tonight the silver moon shivers,
 white frost glitters on hills,
Children sing round a Christmas tree
 that glints in its tinsel frills.

They munch on mince pies by the fire
 watched by a Great Bear* in the sky.
Each window's a stage. As the curtains close
 Christmas Eve must say, "Goodbye".

* The Great Bear and the Archer are groups of stars. The Great Bear is seen only from the northern hemisphere and the Archer is seen only from the southern hemisphere.

Australia – Christmas day

Today the golden sun shimmers,
    orange dust covers the town,
Children sing round a Christmas bush
    that glows in its red-leaf gown.

They picnic on barbecued turkey,
    watch stars draw an Archer's* bow
that quivers, "Goodnight" in an inky sky.
    Christmas day. It's time to go.

Gina Douthwaite

Sophie's surprise

Sophie ran to meet her dad as he came into the kitchen.

"Did you find any letters in the box today, Dad?"
she asked.

"Mmmm, let me see," said Mr Smith. He patted his
jacket pockets.

"Come on, Dad. Where are you hiding them?" laughed
Sophie. Mr Smith pulled out a big brown envelope
and read:

"Sophie Smith, Smith's Sheep Station, Stonycreek,
South Australia."

Sophie opened the envelope. It was from Mrs Hunter, Sophie's teacher. Inside the envelope was Sophie's school work. Sophie lived hundreds of kilometres from the nearest school, so she went to the School of the Air.

Mrs Hunter gave lessons over a two-way radio. There were three other children in Sophie's class, and they all lived far away from each other. They could listen to the teacher and ask questions and talk to each other over the radio.

"I'd like to go down to the box and fetch Mrs Hunter's letters myself," Sophie said to Mum.

"It's too far from the house for you to walk," said Mum. "The box has to be near the road."

Sophie went off to her school room. It was a small bedroom with all the things you need for school work. There were lots of books and paper and paint and the two-way radio.

Sophie knew that the morning's lesson was going to
be about batteries and she had everything ready.
Before the lesson began, Mrs Hunter said,

"We have a new boy in our class this week. His name
is Mike and he's nine years old. At the end of the lesson
you can all get to know each other."

They finished the lesson and soon it was Sophie's turn to talk to Mike.

"Hello, Sophie," said Mike. "Tell me what you do. Do you help your Mum and Dad? How do you get around? I've got a little motor bike. I call it Mike's Magic Machine."

"You're lucky. I don't go too far," Sophie told him. "This morning I got the eggs in and watered the vegetables. If I had a little motor bike, I'd fetch the letters and help Dad with the sheep."

On Friday, Sophie sat down to do her school work. She had to write about the morning's lesson. It was so noisy outside that she could not think. The shearers had come to shear the sheep. There were five thousand sheep to shear, so Sophie knew it would be a long time before they were finished. She went into the kitchen.

"Mum, it's too noisy in the school room. I keep getting mixed up," she said.

"Have a rest," Mum smiled. "Why don't you go to the sheep shed and watch for a while?"

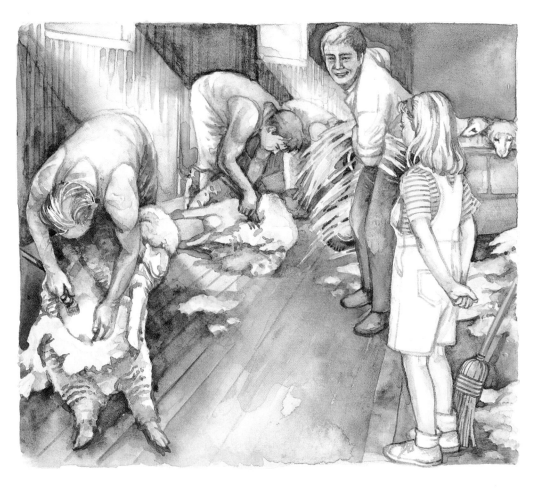

    As Sophie was watching the shearers, she saw her Dad at the back of the shed. He looked surprised to see her and he quickly threw some straw over something near him.

    "Hello, Dad. What are you hiding?" called Sophie.

    "Never you mind," laughed Dad. "Now come and help me to get these sheep into the shed."

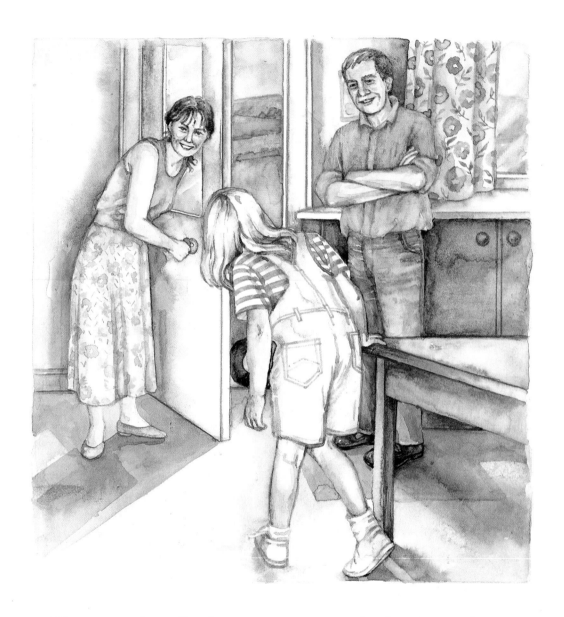

The next day, Dad was waiting in the kitchen when Sophie got up.

"Dad's got a little surprise for you, Sophie," said Mum. She opened the back door.

Just outside, there was a little silver motor bike.

"I asked one of the shearers to get it," said Dad.
"I wanted to surprise you but you nearly caught me
hiding it."

"Oh, thank you, Dad!" cried Sophie. "It's just what
I wanted! I can't wait to tell Mike!"

"I wonder if there are any letters today," said Dad.

"I'll go and see," called Sophie. She got on the bike
and set off slowly along the track.

"Watch out!" she shouted. "Here comes Sophie's
Silver Scooter!"

Kenji and the butterfly

Kenji was not at all well.

"No school today, Kenji," said Mother.

"Lucky Kenji," said his big sister Michi. "I wish I could stay at home. I've got a terrible day today."

"So have I," said their big brother Taro.

"Me too," said Hanako, their little sister. Mother laughed.

"What about me?" she asked.

"And me?" said Father. "Oh, well. We'll all just have to have a bad day today."

Off they went, one by one. Mother and Father went to work. Michi, Taro and Hanako went to school. Grandmother and Kenji were left alone.

"Do you want a book, Kenji?" asked Grandmother. "Or the television?"

"No, thank you," said Kenji. "I'll just sleep." But he couldn't sleep. He thought about Mother and Father, Michi, Taro and Hanako, all having a bad day.

"I wish I could help them," he thought.

He shut his eyes for a while. Then, suddenly, he woke up. He looked at the window. And there, flying in, was a butterfly. A beautiful yellow butterfly. It flew round and round, and then it came to rest on his bed. Kenji looked at it.

"Help them," he said. "Please help them." The butterfly was still for a second. Then it had gone.

Kenji's big sister Michi was at school. She had a school test to do that morning. Michi had worked and worked for the test every night at home. She was sure she would forget something. Suddenly, she looked up. A beautiful yellow butterfly had come to rest by her hand. Michi looked at it.

"I'll be all right," she thought. "This test is no problem." She smiled and started to write again.

Kenji's brother, Taro, was having a bad day too. He was on a school trip. First they had gone on a train, a new, fast train. But now they were up in the mountains.

"Keep up, keep up, everyone," called the teacher. Taro couldn't keep up. His feet were tired.

Suddenly a beautiful yellow butterfly floated by. Taro looked at it. He felt strong again. He ran to catch the others up.

Hanako, Kenji's little sister, had a new teacher. Hanako didn't think she liked him. After school every day, the children always helped the teacher to clean the room.

"I don't like him," Hanako thought. "I want my old teacher."

Suddenly, a beautiful yellow butterfly touched her hand. Hanako looked at it. Then she looked at the teacher. He smiled at her. She smiled back at him, and went to help the other children to clean the room.

And what was Mother doing all day? Well, she had just started work at a new factory, and she was in a terrible mix-up! She had to put a special very small switch into each television set.

"All the others are so clever," thought Mother. "I can't do it."

Suddenly, there was a beautiful yellow butterfly on the next set. Mother looked at it.

"I'm clever too," she thought. "I'll soon learn."

Father had worked late that day. His eyes were tired and his back was tired. He got off the train.

"And now I have to walk home," he thought. "Oh dear, what a bad day I'm having."

Just then he saw a flower shop, with every sort of lovely flower in the window. On one flower, there was a beautiful yellow butterfly. Father looked at it. Then he went into the flower shop.

"It's time to eat," said Grandmother.

"I feel better," said Kenji. "I'm hungry." Then in came Father with lots of flowers, and everyone sat down to eat.

"My test was fine," said Michi.

"And my trip," said Taro.

"And my teacher," said Hanako.

"It was a good day after all," said Mother.

"Why do you think it was?" asked Hanako.

Kenji was looking at the butterfly as it floated away into the night.

"I know," he said.

The world's so big

Think of all the people
I'll never get to know
because the world's so big
and my wagon's so slow.

Think of all the places
I'll never get to see
because the street's so long
and Mother's calling me!

Aileen Fisher